NIGHT
OF
HORRORS

R. Kane

ISBN: 1946577006
ISBN-13: **978-1-946577-00-9**

To my wife and daughter

CONTENTS

RED SPADES

Under the cover of night two men, Ezra and Toby, self-proclaimed expert grave robbers, stroll right in to the cemetery without any effort. Neither seems to notice nor care that there was no gate or any walls protecting the deceased from thieves like them.

They don't even notice the one thing that is very unusual about this cemetery. The graves look freshly dug but the stones are old.

"Do you think someone has beaten us here?" Toby, the muscles of the two asks. "It looks like these people were dug up yesterday."

"Doc told us that this is a great place to find fresh bodies," Ezra smiles. "This should be easy money."

They take out their wooden shovels for a quiet dig and swiftly get to work. Toby sticks the spade in to the ground and it sinks in right up to the handle.

"God, this is the softest ground I've ever seen!"

"Be quiet," Ezra nervously whispered. "You going to get us caught."

They start digging again when they both see a man's face staring up at them. The skin around his mouth has decayed revealing sharp fangs. Ezra grabs the lantern to make sure they aren't seeing things.

"What are you?" Toby asks laughing.

The man's eyes shoot open. With amazing speed he leaps towards Toby who lets out a girlish scream right before his throat is torn out. The blood splashes the lantern light out. The man gets a quick bite on Ezra before turning his full attention back to feeding on Toby.

In a heart pounding panic Ezra runs for his life towards the town below. Looking back he notices several sets of arms popping out from the graves.

When he gets in to town no one is around.

"Help! Someone help me!" Ezra screams pounding on several doors.

A few angry and nervous faces peer out of windows but no one answers their doors.

"Hey, you, come over here," calls a raspy voice.

An old woman waves at Ezra.

He runs towards her and they both go inside the old woman's small home. A fire lighting the room has an uncomfortable effect on Ezra as he looks around and sees different parts of several small animals scattered all over the floor.

Noticing his nervous look the old woman offers him a cup filled with what looks like black tar. He tries to take it but his hand is too shaky to hold anything.

She grabs his arm and looks at the fresh bite wound.

"You have been bite by one of them! What did you do to wake them up?"

"What are they?"

"Bloodsuckers. Vampires. Whatever you want to call them. More will be here soon now. You need to listen to me, unless you want to become one of them."

She starts shuffling around different potions and grabs one.

"You need to cut out the heart of the one that bit you and burn its heart," she says trying to hand him the bottle. "Then you need to mix the ashes with this and drink it."

Ezra looks at the bottle with hesitation.

"NOW!"

Ezra grabs it and runs back toward the cemetery.

The old woman calls to him one more time. "If any others try to bite you, a wooden stick through the heart will kill them."

The old woman turns her back when five fast shadows appear behind her.

"No, you are not welcome in my home! Get out!"

She scrambles to light a candle but when she does five sets of teeth sink in to her neck.

Ezra watches several vampires breaking in to

homes. He turns his attention back getting up the hill.

Back at the cemetery, Ezra watches as the bloodsucker that killed Toby is sinking back in to the ground.

"Here goes nothing," he sighs entering the now almost empty graveyard.

He picks up Toby's shovel and breaks it in half. Quickly he sharpens an edge on one of the tombstones.

Looking around he sees Toby's corpse lying not too far.

Ezra runs over to see his friend. But he looks up to see he's not the only one looking at Toby.

Two bloodsuckers, a man and woman, look at Ezra for a fresh meal.

Out of hunger the man sprints full boar at Ezra. Ezra grabs the new spear and impales him with ease.

The woman moves cautiously around as Ezra yanks the crude spear out of the bloodsuckers chest. This time Ezra doesn't wait for the attack. He throws the spear right through her decaying gut.

She falls to the ground but is not out. She stands up and screams.

Ezra spins the shovel around and chops her head off.

Feeling good about himself and no longer afraid he strides over to the bloodsucker that had bitten him and starts digging.

Using the same spade covered in crimson red, he stabs the man in the mouth. The man yells and tries to move but he is stuck to the ground. Using a pocket knife to finish the job Ezra the heart out.

Holding it up like trophy he rolls back to solid ground when he notices several figures running around him. Before he can move, he is surrounded by ten of them. The fear seeps back in to Ezra who tries to ward them back with the heart. But by then they are already closing in on him.

The next morning a wagon pulls up to the cemetery. On the side is written "Dr. McIvor". Two men get out and look down at Ezra and Toby on the ground. Several bite marks and not one drop of blood near them.

"Good job Doc, another pair of fresh bodies. We have several today."

They are tossed in to the wagon along with several of the townspeople for their final ride.

NOTHING TO FEAR

An old black and white video is playing of President Franklin Roosevelt giving his infamous 1933 inaugural speech before a huge crowd.

"We have nothing to fear but fear itself."

After the speech Mr. Harland stops the video.

He looks out to his science class. On the white board is "WHAT IS FEAR?"

"Okay guys, who agrees with the President?"

No one answers.

"What is the big issue we deal with now in the world?"

A voice speaks up, "Terrorism."

"Exactly, thank you Natalie. Fear is a big part of our lives and we're going to study fear."

He points the projector on the white board. A giant picture of a hairy spider with giant fangs dripping venom.

"Is anyone here afraid of spiders?"

A few hands go up.

"Babies," smirks the class bully Alex.

"Alex, do you mind keeping your thoughts to yourself?"

"Spiders aren't scary."

"That's your opinion. Like personalities, everyone has different phobias. Fear of spiders is arachnophobia. There are hundreds of different phobias, can anyone name another?

"Phasmophobia," said Natalie.

"Good, yes, fear of the ghost."

Alex laughs, "How did you know that? Afraid of ghost Nat?"

"Shut up."

"How about when something traumatic like car wreck?" another student calls out.

"Do you mean post traumatic syndrome disorder? That is different than a phobia but we will look at research being done on the prefrontal cortex section of the brain for PTSD. But to answer my first question, was FDR right? I believe he was. Fear of the unknown is the scariest of all fears. We always imagine the worst will happen to us. In my opinion we have nothing to fear but fear itself."

The bell rings.

"For homework tonight..."

A few zombie groans.

"Write a paper on what you are afraid of. You don't have to share it with anyone but me. It will count as a quiz grade."

Natalie and Alex walk out and their best bud, Pete, starts walking to the lunch room with them.

"What's up guys?"

"Harland is making us write a paper about something we're afraid of."

"That's easy for me, public speaking is the

worst." Pete's face turns red from revealing his fear so easily.

"My grandma's porcelain doll collection always creeped me out. I can't tell her or she'd feel bad. I know how much she loves them. How about you Alex?"

"Just give me a zero now, I have nothing to write about."

Natalie rolls her eyes. "Sure, you aren't. Liar"

"I'm not lying. Maybe I'm missing amydedogala, or whatever it's called."

"Okay, I dare you to spend a night at that abandoned house of First Street."

"What, why?"

"If you are not afraid of anything you should be able to spend a night there."

"No way, that's dumb. I got my own bed, why would I spend a night with druggies or whoever's squatting there."|

"I don't think you're brave enough to stay there all night."

"Shut up Natalie!"

Pete reminds them, "There are two ghosts in there, the boy who went missing on Halloween in 1971 and the woman died drinking bad alcohol during Prohibition from the bathtub. I couldn't do it."

"If you stay there, Pete and I will tell everyone how fearless you are."

"That's hardly an award, everyone knows how fearless I am."

"Fine, we'll do your homework for the rest of the year."

Alex nods his head. "You got a deal."

He heads down the opposite hallway. "Later losers."

"I don't want to tell everyone he's fearless and do his homework."

"You won't, he's all talk."

"I hope so."

Later that night Pete and Natalie are waiting on Alex. They both are staring at their cell phones on the sidewalk across the street from the abandoned house.

Pete glances at his watch. "Where is he?"

"Maybe he's staying home."

Alex jumps out of the bushes. Pete and Natalie scream.

"You two are jumpy."

"Real funny," said Pete.

"I'll have a lot more time for video games after tonight."

"Not yet, you got to spend the entire night."

"I will, going to get a great night sleep too."

Alex takes out his backpack and pulls out a bottle of rum. "I thought I give that old ghost a bottle of alcohol, you know, make up for the last batch she had."

"Where did you get that?"

"My Dad's stash."

"I wouldn't tease these ghost, they might be pissed being stuck in that house," Pete warns.

"Just in case I brought you something."

Pete takes out sage and a lighter to burn it.

"What am I going to do with this?"

"It helps keep evil spirits away. Hopefully you won't need it."

"I don't believe in that junk. I'm more worried

about the crackheads."

"Okay, head on in, we're going to wait til you shine your light in the second floor window. Prove you are all the way in," Natalie tells him with her arms crossed.

"You got it, see you losers later."

Alex heads in, jumping in a window on the side of the house. He turns on his light and sees two glowing eyes staring back at him.

A rat.

"Just great, stupid rat is going to bite me in my sleep."

He heads up the stairs, each one creaking underneath him.

He shines his cell phone light in the window.

Pete waves at him and they both start heading home.

"I bet he'll be sleeping at your place tonight," said Natalie.

"I hope so, I don't feel like hearing about this for the rest of the year."

The first hour went by fast, playing games on his phone. But now the battery was running low. He opens the back of the phone to switch out batteries when he hears a footstep near the stairs. He tries to switch it out fast.

His eyes are starting to adjust to the darkness after staring at his phone. At the bottom of the stairs he can make out a small figure with bunny ears. He gets the battery in and flips his flash light on but no one is there.

"What the hell was that?"

He decides to head up the stairs again to explore.

There are five rooms upstairs, but all the doors are shut.

Alex tries to open the first door, but can't.

"How can someone lock it from the inside unless..."

He starts to knock loudly. "Hey, druggie, wake up! Stupid people."

He turns around and all the other doors are open.

"Hello! Someone here?"

A child in a bunny costume standing behind Alex slowly motions to be quiet.

But disappears before he is seen.

"Hello! Anyone here?"

Not even the rat makes a sound.

At Natalie's grandma's house she takes out her notebook and starts to write.

What fear do I have?

She puts down her pen and walks down the hall. She wraps her hand around the knob. But her hand falls off of it.

"You can do this, don't be such a baby."

In one quick motion she heads in. Hundreds of eyes stare back at her. Porcelain dolls crowd the room. Every shelf and all over the bed. Staring. Their faces freakishly gleam from the streetlight coming in from the window. Natalie tries to breathe normal but is overtaken by her fear. Her ears start ringing, then it turns to babies crying. The screams start to echo throughout the room. She covers her ears but the screeches get louder and louder.

She escapes and slams the doors shut.

The hallway is peaceful and quiet.

Her grandma comes up the stairs.

"Everything okay? I heard a door slam."

"I'm okay. I slammed the door by accident. Sorry"

She wipes her face.

"Okay, don't forget to get your homework done. You said it's about what scares you."

"Yep."

"I'd write about heights, I can barely get up a step stool without getting nervous."

"I'm not sure what I'll write about."

"Don't worry, you'll think of something. Everyone is afraid of something."

Alex takes out the bottle of rum he stole from his parents and goes to the first floor bathroom where the woman died drinking from the bathtub.

"If you are really here, here's some 21st century liquor. Prohibition didn't work, so bottoms up."

In the tub is a smelly brown liquid. Dead flies are floating on top. Some maggots were working their way up the side on to Alex's sleeve.

He shakes them off and stomps one on the floor sending its guts everywhere.

He sits back down on his cot when he see two figures standing at the bottom of the stairs.

He shines the light at them but they disappear until the light falls off of them.

"That's a neat trick."

He goes to do it again but both are gone.

His eye catches a glimmer of light near the back of the house.

A light bulb is swinging in the center of the room giving off a faint green light.

He flips the switch up and down but the lights stays on.

Behind him the bottle he brought smashes against the wall.

"Who's there?"

He walks by the bathroom and a woman is sitting next to the tub, her face buried in her hands. The skin on her arms is decomposing. She slowly looks up at Alex.

"Why are you in my house?" she screams.

Alex runs towards the door but the boy in a bunny costume is waiting for him. The front of his costume covered in blood.

Alex tries to go out the window he came in but the woman flickers in and out of focus, appearing all around him.

"Leave me alone!"

He grabs his backpack and pulls out the sage and lighter Pete gave him.

He howls in agony as long, deep claw marks run down his back.

The woman laughs as he screams.

By a miracle the sage starts to smoke sending her and the boy back up the stairs.

Alex frozen in fear watches the pair stare down, waiting.

The next morning Natalie and Pete get to the house. "Think he's still here."

"I hope not."

They find the window and climb in.

"Alex!"

They hear a muffled voice near the front.

Alex is sitting up, his blood dried on the wall,

the sage burnt to a small nub.

They can see fear in his eyes.

Natalie looks at this back. "What did this to you?"

"Take me home. Please," as tears stream down his face.

They help him up and promise never to come back to the house. Better to leave these ghost alone.

Most importantly they learned everyone has something to fear.

Even Alex.

DEAD MAN'S BELL

Bob Hunt wipes the beads of sweat off his forehead and lets out a sigh of relief. He finally finished digging a fresh grave. He starts climbing out when a hand reaches down to help pull him up.

"Who's there?"

"The name is Jeb, I'm was admiring your cemetery, thought I have something that may be of interest to you."

Jeb, wearing a raggedy hat looks down in to the grave.

"So, are you gonna get out of that hole?"

Bob tosses the shovel up and gets pulled back to

the grass.|

"So you're a peddler I take it. I really don't have much money so you may want to try talking to the Adler family down the hill."

Jeb looks down and laughs. "I don't think they'd interested. I sell primarily to graveyards. Are you burying someone today?"

"Tomorrow. Jeb, I don't have much time.

"Just look and see if anything interests you."

Jeb lays down his bag and places down an odd looking assortment of metal inventions.

"What is this? It all looks like junk."

"Let me tell you. Right here is Grave Bomb. It deters any grave robbers. If they dig anyone up the bomb goes off when they hit the coffin. Is that a problem here in town?"

"No, no grave robbers in this town. What is that thing with the string attached?"

Jeb picks up a small bell on a stake with a long string attached.

"Think how a church bell rings, you just pull the rope. Just tie the string to the supposedly deceased in the coffin. If someone is accidentally buried alive they can just ring this bell and get dug back up. It might not happen often but it can be a nice service to offer. Made these models myself."

"I might be interested in this, how much?"

Jeb turns to around and rubs his hands together. "I have three that I can sell you for twenty dollars."

"Twenty dollars, I may be able to do that. How do I know if they work?"

Feeling he's got the deal in his grasps Jeb figures he's got a great opportunity.

"I will show you. Put me in the coffin and I will show you they work. I'll even take five dollars off for the trouble. Let me just install it on the coffin."

Ten minutes later Jeb is in the dark listening to the dirt being shoveled on his coffin.

"Hey, you don't need to bury me, just put the stake in the ground!"

Put the dirt keeps coming. The coffin is sealed shut.

"Want to be sure it works after someone is buried!"

Bob steps back and sticks the stake in the ground. After a moment the bell starts to ring.

"Well, it works great." He pulls the bell out of the ground. "I can't believe he thought I had fifteen dollars." He picks up the Jeb's bag of wares and heads inside for the night.

SEANCE

Meg drops her backpack and gym clothes on the floor.

Upstairs she can hear a door opening and slamming shut.

"What is going on up there?"

She gets up the stairs and walks into the living room and her parents are both facing the blank TV.

"Hey, what's going on?"

The door stops slamming.

Just silence.

"Hi honey," her mom says to her without turning around. "Did you play with that spirit board with your little friend?"

"Maybe, why?"

Both her mom and dad start laughing hysterically.

"You guys are starting to creep me out. Why aren't you turning around?"

Her mom voice begins to change to high pitch scream. "They've been waiting for you."

"Who?"

Both her parents spin around. Their eyes are nothing but pure white, together they point behind Meg.

Meg screams. Two tall figures are standing at the other end of the hallway. They are pitch black, human shaped shadows.

They surround and wrap around her like a snake.

She tries to scream, she tries to run, but it is too late.

Just silence.

TWO YEARS LATER

Katie Frost, sixteen, is walking home from school in drab clothing. Her backpack has been patched several times but books are still poking out.

A girl chases her down. "Hey! Are you Katie?"

"Yeah."

"My name is Emma. I'm in your homeroom."

Katie continues walking. "Cool. What's up?"

"You know what happened in your house a couple years, right?"

"No."

"What?" Emma exclaims surprised.

"What happened?"

"The family killed each other, a friend of the daughter, Lauren, said they were possessed by a demon!"

"You sound kinda excited about it."

"Nothing like that ever happens here. Murders I mean."

"Well, it was nice meeting you, but I got to get home. See ya tomorrow."

Emma stops and waves. "Okay. Maybe we can hang out sometime."

Katie is already too far to hear.

At the house empty beer bottles with cigarettes butts are sprawled on the kitchen table. A dark yellow fluid lines the bottom of each bottle. Katie's mom is struggling to lean on the counter with a fresh smoke between her bony fingers.

"You're late."

Katie glances at the clock. "Just a couple minutes Mom. Talking to a girl from school."

"You got chores to do," she tells her before taking another puff.

"I know, going out there now."

Katie heads outside is her best overalls. A small sound comes from the bush. A white bird limps out with a thorn in its foot.

"Poor bird. I can help you out."

Very gently but swiftly she pulls it out.

After looking at its foot, the hole seems to have closed on its own.

"What the..."

Before she can look any closer the bird flies away. "You're welcome."

Later that night Katie comes in covered in dirt.

She waves at her mom on the couch. "Going to take a shower."

"Make it quick, water isn't free."

She heads to her room and falls on to her bed. Digging through her side table she pulls out a granola bar and devours it.

The wrapper drifts on the floor.

Katie bends down to pick it up but notices a piece of wood on her floor doesn't quite match the rest.

She steps on it and the board starts to move.

She pulls it up, glancing up to make sure her mom isn't coming.

She nervously puts her hand deeper and deeper until she gets a hold of something.

She pulls up a book.

Filled with confusion and excitement, she wipes away the dust of the book to see the title.

Séance.

"What is this?"

She opens it up and on the top is a name. Meg Taylor, handwritten and a little dark red stain underneath her name. Blood?

The pages have yellowed from age, some starting to fall apart.

She sees more dark red stains on the first dozen pages.

"Time to eat!" her mother croaks.

Katie quickly closes the book and puts it back under the floor for the night.

In the lunchroom ladies are plopping mashed potatoes onto the kid's trays. The cafe is loud with everyone trying to find their friends. Katie is sitting outside when she spots Emma coming over.

"Crap," Katie whispers to herself.

"Hey Katie, what's up?"

"Nothing much."

"I printed you out an article about your house," taking out several folded pieces of paper.

Katie takes the top one with a picture of the house surrounded by police tape.

Triple homicide in home. No suspects at this time.

"Interesting."

Katie can feel someone staring at her.

The distance is a girl in Gothic style clothes. The girl quickly looks away when Katie looks up at her.

"Who's that?" Katie asks pointing towards the girl.

"That's Lauren, the girl that said they killed each other 'cause of a demon. She's crazy."

Katie watches Lauren walk away before disappearing among the crowd leaving the lunch room.

Back at home Katie pops open the floor board and pulls out the book.

The pages seem loose, she realizes that they all come off the binding and that the interior cover is a spirit board.

"Wow, this is neat," she said while examining the board.

She takes her magnifying glass and places it on the board.

"Did a demon really kill the last family lived here?"

The glass begins to move to NO. But immediately goes to the letter S.

"What the...?"

It continues to move on its own, spelling out D E M O N S.

The door behind her slams shut.

The board continues to spell on its own. Over and over again it keeps spelling out W E D I D I T.

Katie closes the board and it flips itself back open.

Katie tries to escape but several shadows wrap around her. And it's too late.

In English class the next morning Katie's head is on her desk, looking into space. Mrs. Patfield, a short older woman comes rushing in. "Morning everyone. Please take your seats and take out your book."

Katie fumbles through her backpack.

"Is there a problem Miss Frost?"

"I cannot find my book," Katie tells her, with a very confused look on her face.

"Well, a three hundred page English book shouldn't be too hard to find. If you don't have it you can borrow one of the extras on the back counter."

Katie gets up and heads to the back of the room grabbing one of the books. Outside the window is the white bird that she helped the other day. The room begins spinning, so much Katie feels like she's gonna get sick.

In the distance she can hear Mrs. Patfield. "Are you okay Katie?"

Katie blinks her eyes, she opens them and her pupils are gone, just white.

She throws the book so hard it smashes the glass

and scares away the white bird.

Katie yells out "Damn!"

The whole class is now standing. She looks at everyone with her normal green eyes. Then faints.

Katie wakes up a bright white room. It's the nurse's office.

A bear sized police officer, school nurse and her mom are staring at her.

Katie looks around. "What happened?"

"You threw the book out the window. No one got hurt but we're concerned about the outburst," the officer tells her. "I'm Officer McDowell. I need to ask you some questions."

"Take her jail, it's what she needs! Straighten her out!"

"Mrs. Frost, I just a need to ask her some questions. Go out to the hallway and calm down." Katie mom finally relents and walks out.

"So, are you on any drugs now?"

"No, I don't do drugs. All I remember is feeling sick."

Looking at the report. "Is this your correct address?"

"Yes."

"I know it can be difficult being the new kid in town. Just be careful out there."

"So, I can go?"

"Yeah kid, just stay out of trouble."

Back at the police station Officer McDowell pulls the file on the Taylor case.

He plays a tape. In a small interrogation room he is interviewing Lauren.

"Why did you go to the Taylor home that night?"

"Meg has been acting funny since..." she pauses with her hands over her eyes.

"Since when?"

"Since we got a book about séances and we thought it would be fun to have one. It got strange really quick. We contacted something evil."

Officer McDowell looks up at the camera and shakes his head.

"So you get to the house, what happens then?" Lauren hesitates, not wanting to live through the moment again.

"The door was unlocked so I let myself in calling for Meg. I went to the dining room and Meg, her mom, and dad were chanting something, I couldn't understand what language. In front of each of them was a knife. When they realized I came into the room they turned and looked at me. Their eyes were all white. They picked up their knife, turned to the right of each other, and stabbed the person in front of them through the cheek. Then started laughing."

She stops.

She can hear Meg's dad's teeth hit the floor in a pool of blood. Then the high pitched laughter.

"They kept laughing as they slit each other's throats open. That's when I called you." Lauren starts to cry.

Officer McDowell stops the interview.

Emma is texting on her phone when Lauren approaches her.

"Hey," said Lauren.

Emma looks around. "Hey."

"I heard what happened to the new girl. Is she

okay?"

"I don't know. She saw something outside and it set her off. I haven't talked to her since it happened."

"Thanks."

"You don't think she possessed do you?" Emma ask with a straight face, then burst out laughing.

Lauren enters a church, most of it already dark except for the small amount of sunlight coming through the stained glass. Long shadows are cast by the statues.

Lauren gets to the front when she hears the side door open.

"Father John?"

"Lauren, what are you doing here?"

"I need to talk to you. A girl that goes to my school moved to the Taylor house. I know you saw something when they asked you to bless the house. I saw you run out."

The young priest rubs his hands together. "Going there is out of the question."

"I think she needs help," Lauren yells. "If you're too scared I will do it myself."

"Don't go there. Nothing good will come from it."

Lauren stops. "This thing killed my best friend, I have to do something."

TWO YEARS AGO

Father John parks in the Taylor's driveway. At the door Meg's mom lets him in.

"Hello Father, thanks for coming."

"Of course. It's always a pleasure to bless one's home."

She nods her head. "Yes."

They head to the living room and three crucifixes are on the dining room table.

"Why don't you hang these on the wall?"

"We've tried. They just keep falling off," she tells him, nervously laughing.

"Where's the rest of the family?"

"My husband is at work. Meg is at her friend's house."

"Well, I won't be long. You have very nice home here."

She nods looking at the floor.

"Is everything okay?" Father John asks.

"We need to get out of this house.

Father John starts to talk but realizes he can see his breath.

"Do you have the air on?"

The three crucifixes fall off the table and break in half.

A deep voice comes from the top of stairs.

"GET OUT PRIEST"

Staring down at Father John are three shadow creatures.

He takes off for his car.

Mrs. Taylor yells out for the porch, "What should we do?"

"Get out of this house!"

PRESENT

Katie is looking through the window.

"What are you looking at?" her mom yells.

Katie doesn't move.

"I'm talking to you!"

"Leave me alone," Katie tells her without turning around.

"Don't tell me to leave you alone."

A horrible laugh pours out of Katie making her mom stops in her tracks.

"Poor woman," comes out as a hoarse whisper from Katie's throat.

A shadow wraps around her mom, giving her just enough time for a blood curling scream.

Then silence.

Katie pulls out her phone and text Emma.

Come over, be good to see you.

Emma walks up the stairs, the door is wide open. She sticks her head inside.

"Katie?"

A hand wraps over her mouth.

It's Lauren.

"What are you doing here?"

"Katie text me to come over. What are you doing here?"

Before Lauren can answer there's a crash coming from the kitchen.

Both girls slowly go in.

Katie is standing in the middle of the floor looking at the drawer of silverware broken on the floor.

"Hey guys, what are you doing here?"

"You texted me to come here."

"I don't think so."

Lauren starts to look around. "Where's your mom?"

"I don't think she's home from work."

"Her car is here."

Lauren runs up the stairs to Katie's room.
"Where is that book Katie?"
Katie follows her and takes a deep breath,
smelling Lauren.
"We remember you."
"What?"
Without warning Katie shoves her down the
stairs sending Lauren bouncing, her leg snapping.
Emma screams from the bottom of the stairs,
"What are you doing Katie?"
Katie eyes are pure white.
The door at the end of the hallway starts to open
and slams shut.
Three shadow creatures are standing, staring at
Emma and Lauren who's writhing in pain.
They start to crawl forward.
"Get back!" Emma cries.
From behind them a bottle a holy water is
hurled, breaking against the wall.
The creatures retreat back, the door at slams
shut. A loud howling shakes the house so violently
it moves the foundation.
Inside the coat closet Katie's mom slowly sits
up, possessed by the darkness in the house.
"We need to get Lauren to the hospital," Emma
tells Father John
Katie struggles to walk down the stairs.
"What is going on? What happened to Lauren?"
"You pushed her down the stairs!"
Father John looks at Katie and makes the sign
of the cross on her forehead.
A knife plunges in to his back. Katie's mom

pulls the knife slowly out laughing hysterically.

"I thought I heard you priest. I can feel your fear."

She licks the blade, almost severing her own tongue off.

She moves in to stab him again when a familiar voice yells ay her.

Officer McDowell has his gun drawn. "Stop!"

She turns and laughing hysterically cuts her own throat, blood turning the laugh into a gurgle.

They move in to save her but it's too late.

A WEEK LATER

Katie is sitting in front of the house with a few suitcases.

Emma and Lauren pull up. Lauren hops out in her fresh cast.

Behind them is Father John.

"Hey guys."

"So, where are you going?"

"My cousins, then who knows. Sorry about your leg Lauren. This whole thing has been a nightmare."

Lauren looks up. "Glad that demon shook the house so hard. Guessing they'll just knock this house down, cost too much to fix."

"You said you had something to give me Katie," said Father John

"Yes, Father, I want to give you this." She takes Séance out of her bag. "I figured you'd be the best person to dispose of this or at least it take it somewhere so no one plays with the spirit board."

"Thank you, I will make sure it is never opened

again. Safe travels Katie," said Father John before driving away.

Officer McDowell comes over the hill in his police cruiser.

"Hi girls, staying out of trouble?"

"Trying," laughs Lauren.

They pack Katie's bags in the trunk and start driving down the road.

Katie looks out the window then looks up. She can see the white bird flying over her. She can only smile at the sight.

Back at the house Emma walks up the porch and looks in the window. "We're going to miss this house."

"We?" Lauren asks, not sure if she wants a response.

Emma spins around with white eyes.

Lauren tries to scream, she can't run, either way it is too late.

Then there's just silence.

MY SANDWICH

Howard sits down at a park bench to finally eat his lunch, a simple ham and cheese sandwich. Regardless how old the ham is he was going to devour this sandwich. He opens his mouth when a small creature, no bigger than a human head, joins him on the bench.

"What are you, a gremlin or something?" asks Howard.

The creature points its boney finger at the sandwich with an innocent look on its face.

"No, this is my sandwich! Get away from me!"

The innocence washes off and is replaced by a sinister scowl.

Not feeling threatened by the little creature, Howard turns to his sandwich and manages to eat the whole thing in one bite. He turns and smiles at the creature while rubbing his full belly. To Howard's surprise, it smiles back.

Feeling a bit uncomfortable, Howard stands up to leave. He turns his head one last time and the bench is empty.

When Howard turns back the creature leaps at his stomach. Howard tries to scream, but his breath is taking away as the creature rips skin and muscle with furious speed. It crawls in and disappears inside Howard's stomach.

Howard begins to gurgle up a bucket of blood when the creature comes out of his mouth. And in its claws is the barely chewed sandwich

"My sandwich," it screeches before darting towards the woods.

FORGIVE AND LET DIE

1941

Two teenagers are hacking down a tree.

"I bet you can't cut down this tree with one more chop."

"I bet I can!"

"Give me a minute," he says rolling up his sleeves.

"Today please Jimmy."

"Hold on to your horse's boy!"

He picks up and swings the ax in to the trunk with all his might.

The tree barely moves.

"I told you."

A pristine 1937 Ford Sedan Delivery car comes rolling over the hill.

The tree starts to fall towards the car...

Present Day

Kevin, sixteen, wakes up for the day. "Crap, gonna be late again!"

He runs down the stairs, steals his brother's waffles and out the door. He can hear his brother yell something but not enough time to stop.

He gets to class but the teacher, Mr. Palmer, is already talking in front of the class.

"Thank you for joining us Kevin," said Mr. Palmer. "Got your late pass?"

"Sorry, yeah," Kevin says handing his slip.

"As I was saying, you will need to do a report on local history, due next week."

Kevin smiles. He loves history as his subscription to any and all history magazines and piles of history books in his room will tell you.

After school Kevin drives down near a construction site. New houses being popped up wherever there's an open field in town. Surprisingly the site is quiet on a weekday, all the building has stopped.

He continues down the dirt road that leads up to a fallen tree. Tangled in the roots is an old license plate.

"Whoa, cool!"

He throws it in his pack and heads to the car.

As he gets closer he notices something on the driver side window.

FIND MY SON written in frost.

He looks around and there's no one but him around.

Considering the hot temperature there's no way there should be any frost.

He climbs in and drives off, the message slowly disappearing.

"Hey, why'd you steal my breakfast this morning?" his brother Frank yells from the door.

"Sorry, I was running late."

"Well I was almost late for work."

He throws his bag on the table and pulls out the license plate. "Check this out."

"You're always bringing home old junk, where did you get this?"

"Up the road, that new construction site."

"I just read about that, they are pulling out, the trucks keep breaking down or something."

"Weird. It'd be good to have a little open land though."

Frank shrugs. "I'm outta here, Mom and Dad will be late. They're going on a date night or something."

Kevin pulls out leftovers when he hears a knock at the door.

"It's unlocked Frank!"

He hears another knock, a little harder this time.

"Are sales people coming this late?"

He looks out the window and no one is there.

He turns but now the knocks are loud enough to break down the door.

He opens it and nothing. He walks out and looks around.

No one.

He goes back in and a woman in 1940's clothing is staring at him.

"Who are you? How did you get in here?"

She writes on the window pane in the frost.

She flickers twice before disappearing.

"Find my son," he reads touching the glass now

frozen like earlier. It quickly disappears as the room temperature catches up and defrost it. But the message remains.

In the school library Kevin looks up the plate number trying to figure out what year it was from.

The volunteer librarian and Kevin's friend Mr. Goulding comes up and examines the plate.

"What do you have here?"

"I found it at a construction site under a tree. Do you know what year it'd be from?"

"Looking at the numbers, I'd say the late 30's, early 40's. Really cool find."

"Is it possible to find the person it was registered to?"

"It's possible, let me talk to friend that can help us."

"That'd be great, I got a local history project due soon and this would be perfect."

"Sure."

"Do you believe in...actually never mind. Thank you for checking that."

"No problem, I'll let you know. Just need a quick picture, and we'll see what we find."

"What's up man?" said Frank while watching TV.

"Mr. Goulding is researching the history on that license plate. But I don't think I should keep it."

"Why?"

"You're going to think I'm crazy. But since I found it I've been getting messages. I think I saw a ghost woman last night in the house."

Frank spring boards off the couch. "What message?"

"Find my son," said Kevin.

"If that ghost is tied to that plate you better find her son or bring it back right now. She will just get angrier the longer you have it without her son. I've seen too many ghost shows on this, she will get you while you're sleeping."

"Are you serious?"

"Yes, go give that thing back."

Kevin rides back to the spot and starts to look around. Before last night he didn't believe in ghost himself.

Under the tree is a rusty piece of metal and an old headlight. He puts the plate back where he found it.

"I put your plate back. Good luck finding your son."

He goes back to car and tries to start it but it won't turn over.

"Just great."

The woman is directly in front of the car. Her face distraught and heartbroken.

Kevin feels a growing pit in his stomach. He knows he is her best chance for help.

"Okay, I'll see what I find. But no more house visits."

The car starts on its own.

Down the road he grabs his phone and calls Mr. Goulding.

"Perfect timing, this license plate has a very sad history. But it'll be great for your book report, can you come down to the library?"

Kevin gets there and Mr. Goulding is at the microfiche looking at an old paper from June 1941.

"Look at this."

The picture is a 1937 Ford Sedan Delivery after being crushed by a tree. The caption reads *Edith Williams, 33, died at the scene. Her son Arthur, 3, was taken to the hospital but his condition is unknown.*

"Arthur Williams. Is there an evening paper that had his condition?"

"I couldn't find what happened to him, but I did find out the two boys who were chopping down a tree that fell on her were charged. They both got so scared they ran away but neighbors brought them in."

"Did they go to jail? Seems like an accident." Mr. Gould scrolls a little more. "Yep, both were sentenced for twenty years but one, James, died of tuberculosis a couple years in."

"Thank you Mr. Goulding. I appreciate it. This is awesome info."
Kevin sits down and prints out the articles.

"What happened to you Arthur Williams?" he mutters to himself.

Late at the library looking through all old newspapers for anything on Arthur he pulls up Edith's obituary and where she's buried.

"Maybe if he did die he'd be buried with her," said Kevin.

He finds the cemetery but there are hundreds of gravestones.

"This will be interesting to find, hopefully the office is open."

Of course the door is locked.

"Mind helping me out now Edith?" he yells.

"Who?" a woman's voice from behind him calls out.

"Hi, umm, Edith Williams. It would be from 1941."

She is kneeling next to a footstone, pulling out weeds, Kevin thinks she could be in her seventies.

"Grass is just growing over my husband grave. Terrible." She leans back, "Edith Williams. Yes, you are close. Are you relative?"

"No, doing a report on local history. You don't happen to know the story?"

"I do. Her son Arthur went to school with my older sister."

Kevin eyes widen. "Really? You don't happen to know where he is today? It'd be great for my report."

"I do, he lives off East Main. Sure he'd like a visitor." She writes down his address on piece of paper. "Didn't you want to see Edith's stone?"

"No, I'm fine. Thank you for this."

Arthur is outside working in a garden when Kevin walks up to him.

"Hello sir, can you hand me those marigolds?"

"Sure."

"Thank you."

"You are Arthur Williams, right?"

"Yep, that's me. Dottie, the woman you met at the cemetery, said you going to see Mom's grave. What got you interested in my Mom and me?"

"Local history report for school. Also I found your license plate and some other parts under a tree where the accident happened."

"That is amazing. It was probably just a baby tree back then. I will tell you my Mom loved her car, it was her business too. She delivered bread to everyone in town. She was really good at fixing that car too. She had to be, she couldn't afford a mechanic. My Dad left us when I was still a baby and she had to do everything."

"I couldn't find what happened to you after the accident. The paper never mentioned it again."

"I got a good cut on my head. You can still see the scar," he says lifting his hair back. 'My grandparents took me and wanted nothing to do with the papers. They were just getting over their daughter passing, they wanted no more attention. They simply didn't answer the door after I left the hospital."

"Would you mind coming with me to spot where the accident happened?"

"No son, I moved past that part of my life long ago. I forgave those two boys, I know it was an accident."

"Just for my report, it'd be cool to have a photo with you at the spot so many years later."

"I don't think so. I don't trust my eyes driving."

"I can take you."

"No," he said changing his friendly tone to more serious. "I told you I moved on."

"What if I told you your mom is waiting for you there?"

"What did you say?"

"Your mom is the one who sent me to find you."

"Sorry, but I don't believe in ghost or anything like that. You live and die, that's it. Nothing else." Kevin just drops his shoulders and climbs back in his car.

Back at the accident site Kevin sits next to the tree and waits.

It isn't long before Edith shows up.

"I'm sorry, I couldn't get him to come. But I did

find him, he survived the accident, just a scar on his forehead. Your parent's raised him."

She points to the tree.

Kevin goes over and starts to dig a little bit before hitting a metal box that has been mostly rusted with jagged holes. Inside are small army figures and toy car.

"You want him to have this."

She nods.

"But you wanted to be the one to give it back to him?"

She nods again. She lets out a scream the trembles the tree.

"I'm going to leave. But I will give this to him."

Before Kevin can leave a car slowly pulls up. It's Arthur.

"She wanted me to give you this," handing him the box.

"Mom?"

Sorrow fills her face.

"Sorry, I couldn't come up here. I had to move on, I had to forgive and move on. You need to do the same."

Arthur starts to look through it. "Wow, these have been here the whole time. They must've fallen out when they towed the car away."

Above their heads a giant branch cracks and breaks.

Arthur shoves Kevin out of the way.

"No!"

The branch crushes Arthur's chest making it hard to breath.

Kevin tries to push the branch off but it's too heavy.

He dials 911 and tells the operator where they are.

Kevin struggles and manages to lift it off. But Arthur's chest has stopped moving.

Several emergency vehicles surround the area.

"Do you need a ride home kid?" the police officer asks Kevin.

Kevin slightly nods.

He turns to see Edith and Arthur ghost happily holding hands.

Then they fade away.